Ghost Stories

by

J.M.R. Meagher

Watermill Press

Printed in the United States of America

Illustrations by Jim Odbert

ISBN 0-89375-800-0

Contents

Contents

The Night Tim Kelly Won Big

Tim Kelly was a simple man who worked as a janitor in a small village. The job didn't pay very much, but Tim always worked hard. He earned just enough money to support himself and his wife, Maggie. Or it would have been enough, were it not for Tim's curse.

The deep, dark problem with Tim was that he gambled. But there was more to the curse than that. He not only gambled two or three nights a week, but he always lost, too. To be honest, he sometimes won a very small amount. But he was never a winner for long. And he never won big. Well, to be honest again, he did win big once. And that is what this story is about.

By now, Maggie was used to seeing Tim's earnings gambled away each week. She had raised her children and fed her family by taking in laundry. She was a good, strong woman, all the better and stronger for having lived with Tim for so long. It took a very patient person to take care of Tim. But Tim was — deep down — a good man, and Maggie knew this. She didn't think of herself as lucky for having Tim. But she loved him. "He's not a bad lot," she used to say. "And he would be a prince if it were not for his curse."

But Tim's curse continued, year after year. There was one good sign, however. After so many years of playing cards, he seemed to be learning how the game worked. Now all he needed was for his luck to change. It was, after all, only a matter of luck.

"I'm not going to quit," he used to say to Maggie, "so I might as well win." Even Maggie could agree with that. If only his luck would turn. And that was just what happened the night Tim won big.

It was a warm, summer evening—a Friday. Tim had just been paid. Friday was one night he always gambled. In fact, on Friday night, Tim didn't even go

*"I'm not going to quit," Tim said to Maggie,
"so I might as well win."*

home to eat after work. As soon as he received his wages, he would go straight to the pub. Once there, he would sit down for a night of cards.

This night was a Friday night like any other, except for one thing. Tonight his luck, like a long-lost son, had come home.

Tim's friends couldn't believe their eyes. Least of all could Tim Kelly believe his own eyes. He couldn't lose that night. At last, he had learned how the game was played. And his luck had turned. Money was falling into his pockets like rain. Everyone expected him to start losing, as he always had. So they stayed in the game and kept losing. No one quit until Tim had won the weekly wages of every man in the house. Because Tim Kelly was such a good man, there were no hard feelings. That night, everyone left happy. And Tim Kelly left the happiest of all.

Tim was halfway home when his curse returned. He was walking past the cemetery when he heard his name.

"Tim Kelly, Tim Kelly, be a good man and join us," came a voice from the cemetery. Without much thought, Tim turned into the graveyard.

"Over here, my man," said the voice.

And then Tim saw them. There were four gray, glowing ghosts playing cards. They sat on the grass and used a fallen grave marker for a table. Terror came over Tim. He wanted to run for his life and money. But he had never turned his back on a game of cards.

The rest of the story is very short. Even on that night, Tim was no match for these gamblers. They had been playing cards for nine hundred years. And they really knew how the game was

*There were four gray, glowing ghosts
playing cards.*

played. In a matter of minutes, Tim was down. His winnings were soon gone. But the curse was back worse than ever. He bet his shoes and socks, and lost. He bet his shirt and pants, and lost. And with that, he walked home. It was a good thing that it was a warm summer night.

When Tim came through the door of his cottage that night, Maggie was still sitting by the fire. "Tonight I won big," he said to Maggie.

Maggie looked at Tim standing there in his underwear. "Sure you did, Tim," she said with a wry smile. "Sure you did."

The Banshee

Some places seem to be more haunted than others. Step into a house, walk down a street, or climb a hill in the country. Most of the time, you feel that you are seeing and hearing all that's there. What you see is what there is. But sometimes you don't feel this way. You feel that something or someone is there. You don't see it or smell it or hear it breathing, but it's there. You feel almost certain.

Of all the places in the world, Ireland seems to be one of the most haunted. It may be the dark, looming skies. It may be the mists which sweep across Ireland's rocky hills. It may be the winds, alive with too many voices to count. It may be the chill in the air which starts anyone shuddering. It may be all of these. And it may be more. There are feelings, too—strange feelings that you are not alone. Something or someone is there—beside you, behind you, inside you.

Of all the ghosts and creatures of the dark which haunt the coasts and hills of Ireland, one is very special to the land. This is the banshee.

When a banshee takes a form, she is

*When a banshee takes a form, she is always
an old woman.*

always an old woman. She wears flowing white robes which blow wildly in the wind. Often she is combing her long, gray hair. The banshee is known best for her piercing, sorrowful wails. The mournful wailing can be heard in the night across great distances. And it always means that someone is about to die. Sometimes, the person who hears the banshee is the one to die that night. Or it may be a loved one who is going to die. The cry of the banshee brings dread each time it is heard. This story begins with the cry of a banshee.

It was March in the county and city of Galway. There were signs that winter was on its way out. But still, the skies were dark most of the day. And the winds and rain brought a terrible chill.

The walls of Mary O'Brien's cottage, this day, were damp and green with mold. She sat by the fire most of the day and long into the night. At midnight, she was nodding with sleep, and the fire was nearly out. She put down her knitting and stood up to go to bed.

Just then, she heard the dreadful wail of a banshee. It filled the room, and it filled the night. Suddenly, the room seemed twice as cold. She shuddered with the chill and with fear. But there was nothing to do but go to bed and hope that she would awaken in the morning. Mary O'Brien slept uneasily that night.

The next morning, she rose early. She lit the fire and waited for it to take away the worst of the night's chill. She had not forgotten the banshee's cry. But she was alive and was glad of that. Perhaps it had just been a gale whistling through the house's many cracks. But she knew

17

better than that.

Just then, there was a knock at the door. "Come in, it's open," she called. The door opened. It was her dear friend, Kate Cregan, coming to visit. Kate looked a bit pale and her smile was weak. They exchanged greetings and sat by the fire for tea.

After several minutes, there was another knock at the door. Mary set down her teacup and walked to the door. It was another neighbor and friend, Maureen Neary. She looked even more pale and upset than Kate.

"What is it?" asked Mary.

"I have sad news for you this morning, Mary," replied Maureen. "Kate Cregan has passed away during the night."

"But that's not possible," said Mary, turning pale herself.

"I know, it just doesn't seem possible

To Mary's surprise, Kate Cregan was gone.

that Kate is gone," said Maureen.

"No, that's not what I mean," said Mary. Maureen looked confused. "You see," Mary continued, "Kate is in my sitting room by the fire." Without another word, Maureen followed Mary into the sitting room. To Mary's surprise, Kate Cregan was gone.

Many years later, the wailing of the banshee was heard once more by Mary O'Brien. She was an old woman, and she knew her time had come. With only a little fear, Mary O'Brien fell asleep that night for the last time. The next day, when her friends came to call on her, they found two chairs and two teacups by the fire.

The Ghost
Sheep and
the Farmer

John Lynch was an old farmer who lived at the foot of a mountain. He and his wife Ellen lived alone. Their five children had all left long ago. The land was too poor to support even the two of them well. But they were more or less content with the life they had made for each other. John and Ellen had one cow and two ten-acre fields—one for pasture and one for potatoes.

Not far from the Lynches' cottage, there were a number of deep caves that were said to be haunted. The children in the area often went into the caves. But they were too frightened to explore the caves very deeply. So the stories of ghosts in the caves were told year after year. No one ever saw anything or anyone that looked like a ghost. But everyone was sure they were there in the caves. One only had to go inside deeply enough to find them.

Besides, how else could anyone explain the sheep? No one in that area had sheep. But nearly every night, the bleating of sheep was heard across the fields. No one ever actually saw the sheep. But everyone heard them. They must belong to the ghosts, the people believed. They lived in the caves, but they grazed at night in the open fields at the foot of the mountains.

For years, John Lynch and his wife had fallen asleep to the sound of bleating sheep. The sound always came from the mouths of the nearby caves. The sound was, to them, as ordinary as the wind. But one day, the old couple woke up to the bleating of a single sheep. It was so loud and frantic that it woke them from a deep sleep. John stood up with a grumble and stepped into his boots. He opened the door of his cottage and stepped out into the chilly morning air. There had been a frost. The ground glistened in the dim, early light. The sun was rising, but it could not be seen through the mist. John could see his breath. He shuddered with the cold.

For what must have been half a mile, John followed the sound of the sheep. The mist was so thick that he could see only ten or fifteen feet ahead of him. But the bleating was getting much louder. So he knew he must be getting closer.

Finally, he came to a deep crevice at the base of the mountain. And there was a sheep with a broken leg, bleating loudly. John climbed down into the crevice. He lifted the sheep to his shoulders and climbed up out of the crevice. The sheep had stopped bleating. It was lying still, slung over John's shoulders. And John carried the sheep back with him to his cottage.

It was not until John set the sheep down in his kitchen that he saw how unusual it was. The sheep was a dazzling white. Its wool was as purely white as

John lifted the sheep to his shoulders.

freshly fallen snow. And it was softer than wool that had been brushed for hours. The sheep looked at the old couple with gentle, knowing eyes. It looked gratefully at John, as he set its broken bone and bandaged its leg.

John carried the sheep out to the shed. He made a bed of hay for it and gave it some water. For weeks, he and Ellen cared for the sheep. Before long, the sheep was walking again.

When the time came to shear the sheep, it stood very still. It gave its wool freely and gladly. And when Ellen made a pair of socks from the wool, they were very special. They were softer than any socks John had ever had. And they never wore thin.

John and Ellen were quite surprised when they saw that their sheep had grown back its wool in several days.

When the time came to shear the sheep,
it stood very still.

Once again, they sheared it, and again, the sheep gave its wool gladly. This time, Ellen made a sweater from the wool. It was the softest of sweaters. And it, too, never wore thin. In several months, the sheep had given up as much wool as a flock of sheep. Ellen made socks and sweaters as gifts to send to all her children.

Then one day, the sheep gave no more wool. Once it was sheared this last time, its wool did not grow back. It began to run away when John or Ellen tried to come near it. It tried to poke holes in the fence around the field.

"It wants to leave, John," said Ellen. "It wants to go back to the caves."

"Nonsense," said John. "It belongs to us now. I will build the fence higher."

Ellen became upset with her husband. She knew he was being greedy. The sheep had paid them back for rescuing it. Now, they must let it go. So that night, she opened the gate to the fence. And the sheep ran off.

When Ellen returned to the cottage, she told John what she had just done.

"Foolish woman," shouted John, and he ran off after the sheep.

John ran straight for the caves. The night was alive with the bleating of a whole flock of sheep. John saw what seemed to be at least a hundred sheep. Each of them was white as snow, almost glowing in the moonlight. Watching the sheep were several ghosts. John saw "his" sheep limping towards the others. Its leg was still weak when it ran any distance.

"Stop," John called out.

At this, the sheep were startled. They ran for the caves. And their shepherds

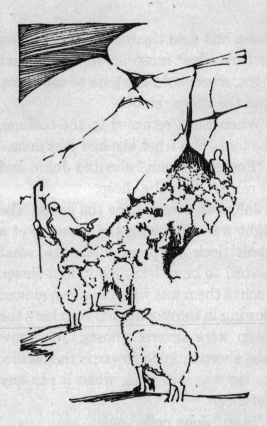

*The shepherds herded the sheep inside
the caves.*

herded them inside. By the time John reached the caves, the sheep were gone. Without thinking, John ran into the caves after them. And he was never seen again.

The Lovers' Leap

A long time ago, there lived a girl named Bridget, who was as fair as any girl you could imagine. But Bridget's beauty became a great problem for her. Every young man in the valley followed her with his eyes and with his heart. And Bridget enjoyed this attention perhaps a bit too much.

Bridget fell in love with a young man, a student named Michael, who loved her madly. Day after day, month after month, they took long walks through the wooded glen that was a favorite place for sweethearts to meet. Soon, they knew every path by heart. Often, they would walk to the Lovers' Leap, a massive rock reaching out over the valley and river below. There they would sit down and listen to the many voices of the river. On lovely summer days when the sun was bright and strong, they would sit on the rock and lose all track of time. It seemed as if their love would grow and grow forever.

Bridget, however, began to take Michael for granted. He lost his mystery for her, so she began to look for someone new. She did not want her first love to die. She only wanted to put it

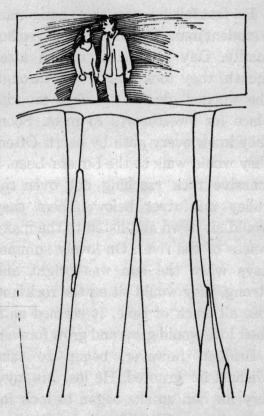

Bridget and Michael would walk to the Lovers' Leap.

aside for a while. And the moment she turned aside, another man, a rich young farmer, offered her his love. Bridget was delighted.

Michael protested. But Bridget told Michael that he was being selfish. He said he loved her more than life itself. She only laughed and turned her back on him.

"I won't be away forever," Bridget said. "We will have more times together." But Michael's heart was broken.

Weeks passed and Bridget enjoyed the attention of her new admirer. They also walked for hours through the glen. And they would also sit at the Lovers' Leap and lose all track of time. There was something lacking in this new love, however. Bridget knew this. She knew that she missed Michael. But something kept her with this new man.

A little while longer, she thought, *a little while longer and I will go back to my true love.*

Meanwhile, Michael was going mad with jealousy and longing for her. He could no longer read his books. He could no longer eat or sleep. His eyes were worn and red from crying.

One day, Bridget went to see Michael. She sighed when she saw what had become of him.

What have I done? she thought to herself.

Bridget realized then that she was being selfish. She told Michael that she loved him and would soon come back to him. But not today.

Michael begged Bridget to stay. But she told him that she had promised to spend the day with the rich young farmer in the glen. The next day,

Michael begged Bridget to stay.

Bridget promised, she would return. But the lovestruck student could not accept this. He said that he had been without her for too long already. He could not live another day without her. "No," Michael told her, "if you leave me again and go to him, I will kill myself."

Bridget only laughed. She knew she shouldn't laugh, but she did. *Michael is just being silly*, she thought. She turned her back and walked away.

And so Bridget spent that day with the rich young farmer. She told him it would be their last time together. That made him sad, but it did not break his heart, for they were not, after all, madly in love. He asked only that they make this last time together a pleasant one.

But Bridget couldn't stop thinking about Michael. Even when she and the farmer were sitting in the sun on Lovers'

Leap, she was thinking only of her true love.

Then, from the village far away, Bridget heard the sound of a church bell. It was tolling for the dead. Each sound of the bell brought a sense of doom to her heart. She knew that Michael had kept his word. He had killed himself. She knew this as surely as if she had seen him do it. And she was right. The young student had killed himself, just as he said he would.

Bridget turned pale as snow. Her eyes were emptied of life. She stood up on Lovers' Leap and looked over the edge of the great rock at the valley and the river below. She thought she would leap. But her companion sensed her despair and held her back. She asked him to take her home.

There Bridget stayed for weeks. She

left her house only at night, to go to the graveyard. Every night, she knelt by Michael's grave. She knelt in the wind and the rain all night without sleeping. Then, in the morning, she would go home. She couldn't sleep or eat. She was going mad. She told her mother that she talked with Michael each night in the graveyard. She said that they would soon be together again.

One morning, after another night by the grave, Bridget told her mother that this was to be the day that Michael would come for her. Her mother was frightened and locked Bridget in her room.

But Bridget waited. At sunset, Michael came for her. He opened her locked door without effort, and they walked out, arm in arm. Her mother screamed when she saw the two of them.

Every night, Bridget knelt by Michael's grave.

"Good-bye, mother," said Bridget as she walked out into the street.

Her mother followed after them. She followed them to the glen. She watched them climb to the Lovers' Leap. She screamed as she saw the young couple leap together over the edge. But only Bridget's scarf fell to the river and was washed downstream. The two lovers vanished into the air. And often, at sunset, Bridget and Michael can be seen walking through the glen and climbing the Lovers' Leap.

Sarge

Ned Doyle was only six years old when his dog, Sarge, disappeared. Ned and his dog were rarely apart, except when Ned was in school. Sarge woke Ned up every morning by jumping into his bed and licking his face. And the two of them walked to school together every day. Ned would look over his shoulder as he ran into school to see Sarge one last time. And after school, Sarge was always there at the end of the lane, wagging his tail. That's why it was so odd and upsetting the day Sarge wasn't there. Ned ran down the lane as always. But there was no sign of Sarge.

At first, Ned thought Sarge was playing a game. Maybe the dog was hiding from Ned and wanted Ned to look for him. Sarge was always full of tricks. And Ned was sure that this was Sarge's latest trick. But there were only so many places where Sarge could be hiding. And Ned tried them all. There was still no sign of him. Ned called out Sarge's name over and over, louder and louder. But there was no answer.

Ned began to panic and ran home for help. He held back his tears as he ran. But when he opened the door of his

Ned called out Sarge's name over and over.

home and saw his mother, the tears poured out. "Sarge is gone," he sobbed.

All afternoon, Ned wandered from house to house and from shop to shop asking if anyone had seen Sarge. The answer was always the same—no one had seen the dog. At sunset, Ned went home and washed for supper. It was a silent meal. Ned ate almost nothing and said even less. No one could cheer him up or take his mind off Sarge. "He'll turn up," was all anyone could think to say. And so his mother and father and his brothers and sisters said it over and over, "He'll turn up." But he didn't. And Ned went to bed without another word.

That night, Ned didn't sleep. He lay awake long after everyone else was fast asleep. Then a distant sound startled him. Far, far away, he heard the yelp of a dog. It was so faint that he thought he was imagining it. Ned listened more closely. Still, he didn't know whether the sound was inside him or was really coming across the fields. Ned's heart was pounding almost loud enough to drown out the yelping. But he jumped from his bed. And, after the moment it took to dress, he was out the door.

In the dim moonlight, Ned ran across the meadow. He still didn't know if he was really hearing anything. But he continued along anyway.

After five or ten minutes, Ned nearly tripped over the figure of a dog. It was Sarge. He was not moving. Bending over, Ned saw that Sarge's right front paw was caught in a trap. It was badly mangled. Sarge was still breathing. When Sarge saw Ned, he tried to get up but fell over at once.

Ned freed Sarge's foot from the trap

and picked him up in his arms. "You're going to be all right," he said. "We're going home."

As Ned struggled to carry Sarge home, he wondered what he had heard. Sarge was too weak to yelp. Maybe the sound had been inside Ned. But it didn't matter now. He had found Sarge.

The veterinarian came and bandaged Sarge's leg. The dog had lost a lot of blood, and he would limp from now on. But the vet thought Sarge would be all right. So Ned slept well for the rest of the night.

But the next day, Sarge was not improving. In fact, he was getting much worse, and his body was shaking with fever. Ned's mother called the vet, and he came at once.

Ned watched as the vet bent over Sarge. The dog's pulse was weak. And he

*The veterinarian came and bandaged
Sarge's leg.*

was burning with fever. The vet turned to Ned. Ned knew already what the vet was about to say. "He's not going to make it," said the vet. "He has a very bad infection. He doesn't have enough strength left to fight it."

That night, Sarge died. Ned and his father buried him behind the house, and Ned went to bed. He cried all night, and the next night, too. He never forgot Sarge. But the pain of losing him grew less with the passing of time.

Three years passed, and Ned was now nine years old. It was an uncomfortably hot July day. Ned had been playing soccer with his friends in the school yard. It would soon be time for supper. As he ran home, he thought it would be nice to cool off. He would be running right by a small pond on his way home. It would feel so good to jump in for a moment, so he did just that.

Ned was not a strong swimmer. He paddled slowly out to the middle of the pond. As he turned to swim back to shore, he felt a pain in his legs. As he fought against the cramp, it spread and grew worse. He screamed for help, but no one could hear. Soon he was exhausted and began to panic. He swallowed some water and started to choke. The awful thought came to him that he was going to drown.

Just then, he felt something grip his arm. It was Sarge! Ned put his arms around Sarge, and the two of them struggled to shore. Ned was afraid that he would drown Sarge, too. But Sarge kept both of them afloat.

When they reached shallow water, they both limped to shore. Ned's legs were still cramped and Sarge's paw was

Ned put his arms around Sarge.

still badly mangled. "Oh, Sarge," Ned sighed, then he collapsed in the grass.

Ned woke up a few moments later, wet and groggy from his close call. He turned to hug the dog that had saved his life. But Sarge was nowhere in sight.

The Coming
of
Billy Deane

"He will come," Annie said, half to herself.

"Who will come, Annie?" her mother asked. She stopped her washing at the big wooden tub. She looked at her daughter and sighed. Unfortunately,

"He will come," Annie said.

she knew only too well who Annie was talking about.

Annie was sitting and brushing her hair in the sun. It shone and sparkled as she tossed her head about. *Her hair is like silk ready for spinning,* her mother thought. *What a beautiful girl she is! But Annie is a willful one, too. She is nineteen already, and still she turns away suitors as if they were beggars at the kitchen door.*

Now, Annie smiled at her mother. "Why, Billy Deane will come, of course."

Mrs. Clare sighed again. Annie had been talking about Billy Deane since she was a little girl. She had first mentioned him on her twelfth birthday.

"The birthday girl must make a wish," her father had said.

Annie closed her eyes and made her wish aloud. "I wish that Billy Deane would come," she said. "I wish that Billy Deane would come and carry me away."

What a strange wish, everyone thought. There was no Billy Deane in all of the village, so everyone thought this was just a girlish game.

Her father laughed. "There's time enough for the coming of Billy Deane — or of any other lad," he added. "A beautiful girl like Annie Clare will be carried off soon enough."

But Annie Clare was not carried off, though it was not for lack of suitors. More than twenty young men had asked John Clare for Annie's hand. She would have none of them.

"I'll wait for Billy Deane," Annie would say. And that was that.

Now, Mrs. Clare wiped the soapsuds from her hands. She sat down by her daughter. "Annie," she said, "it's time you stopped talking about Billy Deane. It was good fun when you were twelve. But you're a grown woman now. You should be thinking of a husband and a family."

"You sound as if you want to get rid of me," Annie laughed. And then she was serious. "Is that true, Mother? Have you and Father had enough of me?"

"Bite your tongue, Annie Clare! No mother and father ever loved their daughter more. But your father and I would like to see grandchildren in our old age. It is a natural thing to wish for."

"Yes, Mother," Annie said. And for a moment, she looked sad. Her mother kissed her.

"There, now. I've made you sad," Mrs. Clare said. "I'll say no more about it."

Annie smiled again and went on brushing her hair. "Don't worry,

Mother," she teased. "Billy Deane will come soon now. And I'll say no more about it either."

Annie was as good as her word. For more than a year, she never mentioned the name Billy Deane.

The following winter was so hard and cruel, the cold and dampness remained well into April. Many people tired of waiting for spring and fell ill. Among them was Annie Clare.

It seemed to be just a head cold, so her mother did all the usual things. She tied a bag of garlic around Annie's neck. She applied mustard plasters to her chest. She made Annie gargle with salt and water, and she held Annie's head over a steaming kettle. Nothing seemed to help, and the cold got worse. Annie soon had a raging fever and became very ill.

A night came that Mr. and Mrs. Clare

*Mr. and Mrs. Clare sat by Annie's bed
and wept quietly.*

were sure would be their daughter's last. They sat by Annie's bed and wept quietly. Annie lay sleeping restlessly. It was then they thought they heard a faint shout, "Hello!" coming a long way across the meadow.

Annie was awake at once. She sat up in bed. "It's Billy Deane!" she cried. "He's come at last."

The shout was heard again—closer this time. Mr. and Mrs. Clare looked at one another and shivered with fear. Annie sprang from her bed as though she had never been sick. The burning fever was gone. The only red in her cheeks now was the pale blush of joy. "I must get ready," she said.

Annie put on her best white dress. She brushed her hair till it sparkled and shone. Then she tied it back with a single green ribbon. "To remember my home," she said.

Annie took a gold locket from the drawer and opened it. Inside were pictures of her mother and father. She closed it and tied it around her neck. "To remember you," she smiled.

There was now a thunder of hoof beats on the road. Another shout, "Hello!" echoed in the night. With a shaking hand, John Clare took his pistol from its place on the mantel.

"Father," Annie said, "it's only Billy Deane, and I must go with him. I've waited so long."

The door was thrust open and a young man stepped into the room. He was tall and very handsome, dressed like a highwayman of a hundred years before.

John Clare raised his gun and fired. This only made the young man laugh. "Father-in-law," he said, "I've come to

A young man stepped into the room.

claim my bride. Is that any way to treat your son?" And he swept Annie into his arms.

In a moment, they were out the door together. There was another thundering of hoofs, and Annie and the stranger were gone. The night and a deadly silence closed around the coming of Billy Deane.

Terry O'Connell's Cat

Terry O'Connell's cat was large and black. "It's good luck," Terry insisted. "A black cat crossing your path is bad luck," he would tell his wife, "but the owner of a black cat has good luck as long as he owns it."

Terry had had the cat since he was a boy. He had found it on a fishing trip one afternoon. He was walking along a river when the cat jumped out of the bushes. It was scrawny and wet. It looked starved, as if someone had tried to drown it.

The cat rubbed against Terry's leg and purred. Terry dried it off, fed it a small fish he had caught, and found himself the owner of a large, black cat. He named the cat Philip.

"Why, this creature is like a member of the family," Terry would say. "There's no telling what our luck would be without Philip."

Whether or not black cats bring their owners good luck is hard to say. But Terry and Maggie O'Connell seemed to have their share of it. Their crops were good. The cow produced milk in great

Terry named the cat Philip.

quantities, and there was always a living for them with a bit of money left over for extras and for savings.

But Maggie O'Connell did not share her husband's feelings about the cat. "It's a dirty beast," she complained time and time again. "It sleeps in my linens, and it scratches my furniture. And worst of all, it leaves fish scraps under the stove that smell terrible."

Secretly, Maggie wished the cat would die. It was surely time enough, she thought. The cat was more than eighteen years old, which was how long it had been since Terry had found him by the river.

Philip, however, showed no interest in dying. He prowled about the countryside at night. He begged for a bowl of cream in the morning. Terry would give him some of his breakfast. And then Philip would curl up in Maggie's linens to sleep for the day.

At three in the afternoon, the cat would rouse himself. He would sharpen his claws on a chair or table leg. And then he would beg for his fish. He would eat greedily all but a few scraps, which he would leave under the stove.

This went on until Maggie felt she could stand it no longer. Then a day came when the O'Connells rose earlier than usual. Terry had business in town. Maggie, having the house to herself, thought she would do some baking. She had the dough ready, and it was rising on a table near the stove.

Philip came in looking for his breakfast. Maggie didn't pay attention to him, being busy with her work. So the cat climbed on the table and walked through Maggie's dough.

Maggie screamed. "My baking!" she cried. "You evil, dirty beast, you've ruined my baking!"

In a wild rage, she seized the cat and headed for the river. "Now you'll go back where you came from," she said. And she threw Philip into the river and watched him disappear.

Terry couldn't believe that Maggie would do such a terrible thing. He ranted and raved at her, then he fell silent and mourned for his cat. He wouldn't eat, and he began to neglect his work. It seemed true — when the cat left, their luck left with him.

To make matters worse, Philip's ghost returned to haunt them. Each night, it would wait till Terry and Maggie were in bed. They would scarcely be asleep when a howling and scratching on the roof would wake them.

At first, they dashed outside thinking Philip had returned. Terry climbed a ladder. Terry could see it clearly in the moonlight. It was Philip, all right. But when he reached for the cat, it vanished.

After a while, they gave up trying to catch the cat. They knew it must be a spirit. Night after night, they just lay in bed listening to the scratching and howling. Maggie knew something must be done. And she was sure she must be the one to do it. It was her evil deed, and she was the only one who could set things right again.

She went to the river and sat on the bank wondering what she might do. She could think of nothing. Filled with despair, she began to cry. "Oh, Philip," she sobbed, "it was a cruel and foolish thing I did. Forgive me, Philip. Please forgive me."

Then she fell asleep on the bank. It was the first sleep she had had in weeks, so she slept deeply. It was late in the afternoon when she returned home. Since she felt better, she made supper for Terry as she used to before their troubles. She prepared biscuits and fish cakes and coaxed Terry to eat.

When they finished, there was a single fish cake left over. She didn't know why, but Maggie took the cake and placed it under the stove. Then she and Terry sat together in silence. It had become their custom. There was no use in going to bed because they wouldn't sleep. They would just wait for the scratching and wailing to begin, and then they would wait for morning. It was always a long time coming.

But this night, there was no scratching and wailing. Both Terry and Maggie

*Maggie took the cake and placed it under
the stove.*

fell asleep and slept soundly. It was the first time for Terry since Philip had gone. And when they awoke, they were ready for a hearty breakfast. "I think I'll work in the fields this morning," Terry said. And Maggie smiled. She wondered how long it had been since she had anything to smile about.

As she was cleaning up after the morning meal, Maggie noticed something. The fish cake she had left under the stove was gone, except for two or three scraps, that is. Perhaps Philip's spirit was ready to forgive her. She filled a saucer with cream and put it on the floor in the corner. Then she ran to the river.

"Oh, Philip," she cried. "Thank you for giving us a night of peace."

When she returned home, she found the saucer of cream emptied and licked clean. And once again, the night passed without the scratching and howling.

Maggie was now sure she was coming to terms with Philip's ghost. One more trip to the river might do it. She left a piece of fish under the stove and hurried off.

At the river, she spoke as before. "Philip," she said, "it's good of you to forgive me. I'll never hurt another creature as long as I live."

Again, she felt better. And it was such a beautiful day that she decided to walk along the river before returning home. She had not gone far when a large, black cat jumped out of the bushes. It purred and rubbed against her legs. Maggie was beside herself with delight.

"Philip! You're not dead after all! We must have imagined everything. Come, I'll take you home to your master. He'll be glad to see you. Oh, Philip, you have forgiven me."

But as she stooped to pick up the cat, it disappeared. This gave Maggie a terrible fright, and she hurried home to tell Terry what had happened.

When she arrived, Terry was sitting in his favorite rocking chair. He was smiling happily and staring into Maggie's linen chest. There, on her best linens, was Philip.

Well, she thought, *real or ghost, we're back where we started. And that's probably where we're best to be.*

No one was ever certain if the cat was the old Philip, a new Philip, or Philip's ghost. But whatever it was, it stayed with the O'Connells for the rest of their lives. That was forty-seven years to the day, which is a long time indeed for a cat.

There, on Maggie's best linens, was Philip.

Terry and Maggie died together on a Tuesday. Philip was found dead by the mourners on Wednesday. He was buried quietly, and was never seen or heard from again.

The Walking Gallows

In Ireland, many lonely spots are said to be haunted by ghosts from the past. Of all such spirits, none is more dreadful than the ghost of Hempenstall, the "walking gallows."

In life, Hempenstall was a terrible

figure. He was a giant of a man, well over seven feet tall. His arms were as thick as fence posts. It was said that he could lift a horse. Men of great strength are often known for their gentleness— but not Hempenstall. His cruelty was a legend throughout Ireland.

By the closing years of the eighteenth century, the Irish rebellion against the British had failed. Under their leader, Michael Dwyer, the defeated patriots had fled to the Wicklow Mountains, south of Dublin. Even today, it is a wild and lonely place. The Wicklow Mountains are a mixture of woodlands and moors, with few roads. But in Michael Dwyer's time, it was a wilderness. There, with his followers, he hoped to escape the British troops who were hunting him down.

The British had other ideas. They

Hempenstall was a giant of a man.

made a road through the mountains so that troops could be moved swiftly. All along the road, they built a chain of forts and barracks. In this way, they hoped to control the movements of the rebels.

The rebels caught by the British were hanged. The wooden frame from which they were hanged was called a gallows. But at Drumgoff Barracks, the British needed no wooden gallows. They had Hempenstall for a hangman. When the noose was tight around the neck of his victim, he would hold him in the air with one hand. That was why he was known as the "walking gallows."

As a result, Hempenstall was a deeply hated man. There were many attempts on his life. But he was not the easiest man in the world to kill. Many people dreamed of killing him. But no one could do it — until one fateful night.

A group of survivors from the rebellion planned to murder Hempenstall. They waited for him by the gate of the British fort. There was a chilling drizzle, and the rebels shivered from the cold. Only a sliver of the moon shone through the clouds.

The rebels waited in the shadows until almost midnight. Sentries passed by every ten or fifteen minutes. Each time, the rebels feared they would be found out. There were only four of them. If they were seen, they would have had no hope against all of the British troops in the fort. And if they were caught, they would hang, one by one, from Hempenstall's arm.

The rebels had watched Hempenstall's moves for weeks. They knew that he took a walk each night at midnight.

And, he drank a great deal. By midnight, his eyes had a thick mist over them. That would be the perfect time to make their move.

Now they could barely see him coming their way in the darkness. He walked like a ship rocking at sea, heaving from side to side. The four rebels groaned at the same time. He was truly a giant! And he cast a shadow the size of a house. Hempenstall muttered to himself in the night. His deep, booming voice was like a bull's. It seemed as if the ground were shaking under his feet. The rebels wondered if they had made some mistake. Could they possibly bring down this hulk of a man?

Hempenstall was only fifteen feet from where they lay waiting. "Now," their leader whispered. And they sprang into action. Two of the rebels ran at

*Two of the rebels ran at Hempenstall
with long swords.*

Hempenstall with long swords. They were on him before he knew it. They swung their swords. *Thwack! Thwack!* He fell like a great oak and thudded to the ground on his back. The cry that came from his mouth was enough to frighten all the ghosts in Ireland. Then he was as silent as a felled tree. The "walking gallows" would never walk again. He had hanged his last rebel.

By this time, the alarm was out. The British soldiers streamed from the fort like a raging river. But the rebels had vanished into the night. The great hulk of Hempenstall lay at the gate of the compound.

For days after, British troops marched up and down the army road through the Wicklow Mountains. They searched the woods and the nearby towns for rebels. But they could not find any trace of

Hempenstall's murderers.

The death of Hempenstall brought no great sadness to the British. He had not been a lovable figure. And they could easily build a wooden gallows to replace him. But his death brought some gladness to the rebels. He had been a curse to them.

As for Hempenstall himself, he is said to appear now and again at the gates of the fort. Even in death, he stands well over seven feet tall. And he carries a heavy rope over his shoulder.

The Long Spoon

Early one morning, a tax man was walking along a road—all alone. This was not surprising because the tax man was not well liked by anyone. He had wrung the last penny out of widowed women, and he had left poor orphans poorer than before. Wherever he went, he went alone.

The man walked on a bit, then stopped in a small grove of trees by a field. The wind was whistling through the woods. This was strange because there was no wind elsewhere. All around him, the sun was shining and the air was calm. But here in the woods, it was dark, and the wind made everything quiver.

The tax man sat on a stone and looked around him, as if he were waiting for someone. He didn't wait long.

Suddenly, the wind died down as a man dressed in black stepped out from behind a tree. Believe it or not, it was Old Nick—the devil himself. The tax man jumped up.

"I didn't think you would come," said Nick. "You had more than your share of punch last night. I thought you might change your mind this morning—so many do, you know."

*A man dressed in black stepped out
from behind a tree.*

"Not yours truly," the tax man said. "We made a bet last night, and I plan to see who wins."

Old Nick twitched his horns under his top hat. "All right, then," he said, "let's go over the bet again. That way, there'll be no mistake over what we are doing."

"Good enough," the tax man said, and he took his seat again on the stone.

"We'll travel together today," said Nick, "until sunset, when we'll see which of us has picked up the better load. But, mind you, we must take only what people freely give us. The gift must truly come from the heart."

"Agreed," said the tax man. "I don't get many offers, but I guess it's the same for you, too."

Old Nick sighed and nodded his head.

"At least, we're well matched," the tax man smiled, "so let's get on with it."

They moved out from the trees and walked along the road. The first place they came to was a small cottage. The windows and doors were open, and they could hear a mother scolding her lazy daughter.

"Jenny, you are such a good-for-nothing child! May the devil take you, you lazy thing."

"Well," said the tax man, "there's one for you, Nick, right at the start."

"No," said Old Nick, "she did not say it from her heart, so we must go on."

Soon, they came to an old farmhouse where the wife was in the yard, calling angrily to her husband inside.

"Ahh, Patrick, you old fool! You never locked up the pigs last night, and now they're digging up the whole pea patch. The devil take them all!"

"Well, Nick, there's another one for

you," the tax man exclaimed.

Nick shook his head. "She's only using a figure of speech," he explained. "She doesn't mean a word of it."

"People certainly say a lot of things they don't mean, it seems," the tax man sighed.

"That's the truth," said Nick as he shook his head again and twitched his horns.

The two went on all day like that. Sometimes a farmer would complain about his wife, or his horse, or his lazy, no-good help. Other times, a wife would nag her husband or one of her children. And still other times, a young man might be taken in by a fickle girl, or a young girl would run out of patience with a timid man. Many times, the devil heard these people call his name.

But whatever it was, Old Nick just

shook his head and passed them by. "Their offers are not from the heart," he said.

The tax man was worse off. No one even talked to him. By the end of the day, no one had offered him so much as a glass of milk.

"It looks as if the well has gone dry for both of us," the tax man said finally. The sun was now only a thin slice above the trees.

At last, the two were passing a house where an old woman was outside draining her potatoes. She looked up and saw the pair.

"Arrggh," she exclaimed, "it's the tax man. I hope the devil runs away with him!"

"Well now," Old Nick laughed, "I've got a bite, at last."

"Oh, come now!" cried the tax man.

"Arrggh," the woman exclaimed, "it's the tax man."

"I'm sure she didn't mean it from her heart. It's only a figure of speech."

"No, indeed," grinned Nick. "It comes from the very bottom of her heart. So, in you go." He opened the mouth of his black bag as the last rays of the sun touched the tree tops.

And that was the last ever seen of the tax man. It was a small loss, folks say about it. Yet even today, they think of the tax man when anyone says, "Whoever eats with the devil must have a long spoon."